Tally & Squill

In a Sticky Situation

Abie Longstaff

Illustrated by James Brown

L B

LITTLE, BROWN BOOKS FOR YOUNG READERS

First published in Great Britain in 2016 by Hodder and Stoughton

1 3 5 7 9 10 8 6 4 2

Text copyright © Abie Longstaff, 2016
Illustrations copyright © James Brown, 2016

A CIP catalogue record for this book
is available from the British Library.

ISBN 978-1-5102-001-42

Printed and bound in Great Britain
by Clays Ltd, St Ives plc

The paper and board used in this book are
made from wood from responsible sources.

MIX
Paper from
responsible sources
FSC® C104740
www.fsc.org

Little, Brown Books for Young Readers

Part of Hodder and Stoughton

For Rebecca Lisle — may every writer

have an author buddy like you.

— A. L.

For my neices, curly-wurly Lucy

and twirly-whirly Freya.

— J. B.

The Secret Library's Rules:

There will be only one Secret Keeper
in each generation.

The Secret Keeper must be
under the age of thirteen.

The Keeper must guard the secret of
the library and the information within.

Talking is permitted.

CHAPTER ONE

Tally lived in a beautiful
old mansion called Mollett
Manor.

It had fairy-tale turrets and
splashing fountains.

It had fancy ballrooms and four-poster beds.

It had secret passages and hidden doors and an
ancient stone circle in the garden.

But if you wanted to find Tally you would have to
go down the tapestry corridor, past the ballroom,
through the servants' hall, into the kitchen, to the
scullery.

For Tally was the servant girl. She slept in the largest of the three scullery sinks.

She was the one who dusted the turrets and cleaned the fountain.

She polished the ballroom floor and ironed the silk sheets.

She was the smallest and lowliest member of the household.

And she was also the most clever.

Where this brilliance came from, nobody knew. Because nobody knew quite where *Tally* came from, not even Tally herself.

She knew her name was Tallulah. She knew she was ten years old. She knew she had once lived with her mother. She even remembered bits of her past — the jangle of Ma's bracelets, the sound of her singing her favourite song, the feeling of being snuggled up listening to a bedtime story. But Tally didn't remember her mother's name. She didn't know where she had been born, and she didn't know where her mother was now.

'Dead,' Mrs Sneed would say, whenever Tally asked. Then the housekeeper would give a cross sniff as if looking after Tally was a lot of trouble.

Mrs Sneed had found her eight years ago, when Tally was only two. She complained to Tally almost every day about what an inconvenience it had been.

'Your wailing made me walk all the way down the garden,' Mrs Sneed grumbled, each time she told the story. 'All the way across the lawn, all the way through the forest and all the way to the sea. And there you were, snivelling, right on the edge of the cliff. So selfish and thoughtless! You weren't even doing anything useful.'

Tally could recall the feel of the wind that day, whipping her pinafore against her legs. She could still picture the crumbling rocks. There was something else she saw in her memories: her mother, dancing, with shining eyes.

'Oh, it's so magical here! One day you'll get to

see it, Tallulah! Thousands of books, just like I told you!' Ma ruffled Tally's baby curls and sighed. 'We can't stay much longer, sweetheart. We're not really supposed to be here. Come on. There's something I need to get from the cliff. Then we'll sneak back out through the hole I showed you in the wall ...'

Tally remembered warm hands setting her down. She clutched her little teddy bear. 'Just sit there,' a soft voice said. 'I'll be back in a moment, darling.'

The rest of the memory came in flashes:

a stumble

a scatter of pebbles

the lace hem of Ma's skirt snapping in the breeze, then disappearing ...

Tally's fingers reached out.

But all that was left of Ma was a scrap of lace in Tally's hand and a handmade teddy on her lap.

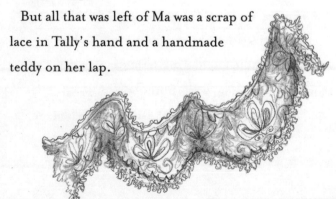

'Ma!' Tally cried and cried.

The sound of footsteps, then ...

... a woman with narrow eyes and pinched lips staring down at her.

'Ma gone!' little Tally sobbed.

'So? What am I supposed to do with *you*?' The woman tipped her head to the side and cracked her long neck.

Creaaak craaaack!

'Come with me,' she sighed. 'I may as well find a use for you.'

Tally held out her arms to be carried but the woman jerked away.

'You have feet, don't you?' she snapped. She picked up Tally's teddy and flung him over the cliff. Then she turned on her heel and marched back to the manor house, leaving Tally to toddle after her.

That was Tally's last memory of her mother, and her first memory of Mrs Sneed. Since then she'd been living at Mollett Manor, home of Lord

Edward Mollett and his sister, Beatrice.

Mrs Sneed had put Tally to work straight away. Dusters were tied to the bottom of her feet so that every step she took could be useful. As soon as she was old enough to reach the countertops she was given a cloth to polish them. By the time she was three years old Tally woke every day to a long list of duties.

Nowadays, Tally did almost all the work around the manor, washing and cleaning and fetching and carrying. She'd never been to school and never played with other children. No one outside the manor knew she existed.

Monday morning, Tally was busy as usual. Mrs Sneed and Mr Bood, the butler, were in particularly mean moods. They'd set Tally the task of cleaning the entire mansion. As Tally filled her bucket in the kitchen sink, they were competing to be the bossiest. Mrs Sneed snapped in her spiky voice and Mr Bood

14

boomed in his deep
voice. Mr Bood
could never
remember
Tally's name. Even
now he was struggling.

'Tilly … er … Tooley!' he bossed.
'Scrub the cloister!'

'Tally!' snapped Mrs Sneed. 'Polish the door
hinges!'

'Twolly!' Mr Bood boomed. 'Tidy the study!'

'Tally!' cried Mrs Sneed. 'Sweep the ballroom!'

Boss, boss, boom. Snap, snap, yap, all morning
long. Tally sighed as she carried her bucket through
the kitchen. Nothing she did was good enough.
No matter how hard she worked, Mrs Sneed and
Mr Bood were still going to grumble. On days like
this, Tally missed her mother so much. She missed
'Well done, darling' and 'I'll kiss it better' and
'Goodnight, sweetheart'. Most of all she missed

15

'Shall we have a story?'

Where was Ma? Deep in her heart Tally knew Mrs Sneed was wrong. Ma wasn't dead. She couldn't be. But what had happened to her? Where was she now? Why hadn't she come to find Tally? Tally shook herself to clear the questions away.

As she scrubbed the cobblestones in the cloister, Tally imagined Ma was sitting right beside her. 'Once upon a time ...' Ma said, inside Tally's head. Imagination was Tally's secret power. She could endure all her boring jobs because her thoughts were whirling and buzzing and bouncing and fizzing. Her mind put on shows, telling stories, singing secret songs and playing with words and pictures. All this happened while Tally was sweeping the pond or dusting the trees.

Ma had loved stories. She used to tell Tally about Peter Pan in Neverland and Mowgli in the jungle. Even though Tally had been really little, somehow the tales had stuck fast in her brain. She could picture the pirates as she polished, or hear Baloo's voice as she mopped. Sometimes Ma had even made up her own tales. They were funny ones about a bear who escaped from the zoo and got up to all kinds of fun. Ma used to draw pictures of the bear wearing different hats as he became a train driver or a fireman. She'd made Tally a little cloth teddy to be Mr Bear, and he'd bounce up and down growling 'I'm off on an adventure!' Well, he did until Mrs Sneed threw him over the cliff.

'Tally!' came a spiky voice from a window above her. 'I told you to polish the door hinges.'

Tally gave the cobbles one last wipe and went back inside the manor house. She picked up her duster and rubbed at the dull brass hinges until they sparkled. She could see her face in the shiny metal now — a head of dark curls, a flash of green eyes.

She carried her bucket along the hallway and up the stairs to Lord Mollett's study. Lord Mollett was a very important writer, his sister said (over and

over again). He had once written a book called
THE HAIR STYLES OF POISONOUS SPIDERS: A thorough analysis.

Now he spent most of his time drinking coffee and staring out of the window.

Tally dusted the glass cabinet outside his room. It held his favourite ornaments. There was a set of cufflinks and a tiny silver bear, an old pocket watch and a diamond ring. There was even a funny brooch made out of a bit of sea glass. It was in the shape of a spider's body and it had spindly wire wound round it for legs. *I wonder why he's kept it?* Tally thought, peering through the cabinet. The spider didn't look smart and expensive like his other things.

Tally quietly opened the study door. *Phew!* His Lordship wasn't there. Tally wasn't supposed to talk to the lord and lady. She was supposed to stay in the background, unseen, to zip in and out of rooms, dusting and polishing. She gave the red wool rug

a shake and plumped up the cushions on Lord
Mollett's reading sofa. Then she cleared a large pile
of half-drunk coffee cups from the window sill and
turned her attention to his desk. She sharpened
all of Lord Mollett's pencils and tidied up the
newspapers. She read the headlines as she went:

CRIME SOARS IN VILLAGE!
Soap stolen from chemist – thieves make a clean getaway

Tally lifted a heavy book to dust underneath. The
cover had a picture of a spider with eight hairy legs,
and a scorpion, also with eight legs, and a long
pointy tail. **ARACHNIDS** was the title on the front.
Tally sounded the word out slowly. *An arachnid must be
a kind of animal*, she reasoned. *One with eight legs.*

As she swept, the book fell open in her hand. She
couldn't help glancing towards the page. Tally's
eyes widened as she read that spiders don't
smell with noses. Instead, they have
scent-sensitive hairs on their legs.

19

There was a little footnote[1]
explaining more about it.
Tally's eyes darted to
the doorway, her heart
beating fast. The hallway beyond was
empty. Tally breathed a sigh of relief. She wasn't
supposed to know how to read. Mrs Sneed regarded
reading as dangerous — it would give Tally IDEAS.

'I never learned to read and it hasn't done me any
harm,' Mrs Sneed would say. (Tally knew this wasn't
true. One time she had seen Mrs Sneed put her head
in the oven and nearly burn it by not being able to read
the label on the oven that said 'Do not insert head'.)

Secretly, over the years, Tally had taught
herself to read. She'd practised a letter here,
a word there, starting with labels on bags of
flour and instructions on cleaning bottles, and
graduating to whole pages of Lord Mollett's
books and newspapers. Tally had learned all kinds
of fascinating things. From an envelope, she'd

[1] This is a footnote. Footnotes are little extra pieces of information
found in books.

even discovered that Lady Mollett's full name was Beatrice Ursula Mollett.

So her initials spelled:

B.U.M.

Tally turned her attention back to the book in her hand and read about the different patterns in spider webs. The duster hung limply from her hand, forgotten. Then suddenly:

'Where is that girl?' screeched a voice from downstairs.

'Oh!' Tally jumped and knocked a pile of magazines off the desk. 'I'm ... er ... here. I'm just tidying!'

Tally put the book back and hastily began dusting again. Her duster paused over more books bound in leather, begging to be read. She stroked her fingertips over the embossed titles. Would she ever have books of her own? A thought tugged at the back of her mind. Books ... thousands of them ... But where? No matter how much she concentrated, she couldn't call to mind a picture of them.

'Hurry up!' barked Mrs Sneed. Tally could hear angry footsteps marching up the stone stairs.

'Coming!' Tally called back, giving the book one last sweep of the duster.

By the end of the day, every bone in Tally's body ached. After she'd finished dusting, Mrs Sneed had made her clean out all the fire grates and Mr Bood had ordered her to polish the marbled floor of the ballroom with a toothbrush. Now she was so tired all she could do was chew a bit of stale bread and jam and climb into her sink to sleep.

As she tried to get comfortable between the taps, she could hear Mrs Sneed and Mr Bood in the kitchen, finishing off the leftovers from the grand dinner Tally had cooked for everyone else. She listened to them crunching on perfect crispy roast potatoes and gorging on creamy leeks, and clamped her hands over her belly as it let out a loud rumble.

'Did you hear about those burglaries in the village?' Mrs Sneed asked Mr Bood, as she scraped a fork across her plate.

There was a splash as Mr Bood refilled his wine glass. 'Farmer Miggins told me they crept in last night and poached some eggs.'

'Poached some eggs?' Mrs Sneed echoed. 'Now, there's brazen for you. You wouldn't have thought they'd have the time.'

'What?'

'Poached eggs take six minutes. I've seen Tally do it.'

'Don't be a nincompoop, Mrs Sneed,' Mr Bood exclaimed. 'I mean poached as in *stole* – they stole the eggs.'

'Oh! I'll thank you not to call me a nincompoop, you nincompoop,' Mrs Sneed replied. There was a scrape of a chair as she rose sharply.

'Well, don't call *me* a nincompoop, you blockhead.'

Tally heard another scrape of a chair and the sound of their bickering voices as they left the

23

kitchen and all the dirty dishes for Tally to clear up in the morning. Their footsteps faded away as they walked to their rooms. She wriggled, drawing her feet up to find a better position against the cold enamel of the sink.

Everything fell silent. The moon shone bright through the scullery window, sending long, pale shadows across the stone floor. Tally clutched tight to the only bit of her mother she still had – the tiny scrap of lace from Ma's skirt. She closed her eyes and made a wish on the moon. 'I wish,' she whispered, 'I wish someone would tuck me in and read to me.' She waited a moment, just in case. Just to see if her wish would come true.

There was a scuttling sound of tiny claws on tiles. A mouse was running across the kitchen.

Crash!

Tally's eyes shot open. She waited a moment, but all was quiet again. The mouse must have knocked something off the table. Tally pulled her thin blanket over her shoulders. Maybe one day, she'd

see her mother again. Maybe ...

CHAPTER TWO

Splash!

Tally jolted awake as cold water drenched her.
Mrs Sneed had turned on the taps over Tally's sink.
Again.

'Up, up, up!' snapped the housekeeper. 'There
you are, not doing anything useful.'

Not Being Useful was a grave offence in Mrs
Sneed's book, along with Having Ideas.

Tally had been dreaming. In her dream she
was somewhere strange, somewhere dark and
mysterious. There were thousands of books and
Ma was there too, sitting at a little desk, drawing a
picture of Mr Bear wearing an explorer's costume.

'I'm off on an adventure,' he was growling. Then the water had shocked her awake.

'What's happened? What is it?' Tally asked, shaking the cold water from her curls as she climbed out of the sink. It was still dark outside the scullery window. Dawn hadn't broken yet.

'There's been another burglary,' said Mrs Sneed, her eyes wide.

'Oh no!' By the light of the lamp, Tally hastily pulled on her starched grey pinafore and cap. 'Where?'

'Here!'

'At the manor?' Tally was shocked. Her mind went straight to the crash she'd heard last night.

'Yes. Lord Mollett's cabinet was broken into and his mother's diamond ring was stolen.' Mrs Sneed brought her face close to Tally's. 'Mr Bood says no windows or doors have been forced, so it might be an inside job.' Her eyes searched Tally's face. 'You wouldn't know anything about it, would you?'

'No!' Tally pulled on her holey grey socks. She tried not to think about how she'd pressed her nose up against Lord Mollett's glass cabinet only yesterday. She swallowed hard. Would her prints still be there?

Mrs Sneed finally looked away, cracking her neck from side to side.

Creaaak craaaack!

'Go and get some kindling from the forest,' she said. 'I want all the fires lit right away.' She glared at Tally. 'The lord and lady need warming up after the shock.'

'Yes, Mrs Sneed.' Maybe Tally could look for clues while she was out. Then she'd be able to prove she'd had nothing to do with the theft.

Mrs Sneed folded her arms. 'Don't you dare enjoy yourself on the way,' she warned.

'Mrs Sneed,' Tally said, 'it's cold and dark outside. I'm drenched in freezing cold water. I don't think I'll be enjoying myself at all.'

Mrs Sneed's brow furrowed as she thought about that. Then, finally . . . 'No singing,' she added.

'Yes, Mrs Sneed.' Tally pulled on her shawl, and headed towards the kitchen door.

Off she went, carrying her lamp,
through the scullery

into the kitchen

along the servants' hall

out the side door

across the cloister

through the rose garden

past the beehives

and deep

deep

into the dark forest.

*　*　*

It's not so bad, Tally told herself as she blew on her
fingers to warm them. *The sun will come up soon.* She
tried to distract herself from the cold by thinking
about the burglary. Who could have forced their
way in to Mollett Manor? Was it the same people
who'd stolen from the village shops?

Tally frowned. She hated the thought of a burglar
getting into the manor. Even though she disliked
Mrs Sneed and Mr Bood, Tally loved the old house.
Long ago, the manor used to be a monastery and
there was something truly special about it. It felt as
though there was a deep magic hidden in its walls.
Sometimes, in between her chores, Tally would
stop, close her eyes and picture the monks moving
about the cloisters in the olden days. Many of their
ancient buildings were still standing. There was
the malthouse, where they used to make ale, the
infirmary, where the monks had been taken when
they were ill, and the old stables, where the horses

31

were kept. Their refectory, where they'd eaten their meals, was now the kitchen but the apple orchard survived and the beehives continued to be busy with bees making honey.

Tally's favourite thing about the manor was its secret passages.

The monks had made them hundreds of years ago and each one was unlocked by solving a puzzle or a code. Some of the puzzles were really hard. The key to the passage from the drawing room to the red bedroom had taken her ages to figure out.

Over the fireplace in the drawing room was a picture made of wooden blocks, each one with a number on. It looked like this:

Tally had cleaned it every day for years before she realised that the blocks could be moved. She'd shifted the numbers randomly around and around. Then one day she saw an old book in Lord Mollett's study. It was called **MAGIC SQUARES** and it was full of puzzles where in every row, every column and every diagonal, the numbers had to add up to the same thing. Tally had rushed back to the drawing room and stared at the wooden picture.

All the numbers added together made 45, she worked out. And there were three rows and three columns. That meant, to make a magic square, each row and each column had to add up to 15. Tally moved the pieces around until she found:

As she'd slotted in the last wooden piece (number 9), a secret door in the fireplace had clicked open and Tally had whooped for joy. Another code solved!

Mrs Sneed and Mr Bood had no idea that the hidden passages existed. Tally had never seen them use any of the shortcuts that led across the grounds, and she certainly wasn't going to give away the secret. The passages were very useful to hide in when she wanted a few moments of peace.

Now, Tally frowned as she searched for more kindling. Surely the burglar couldn't have figured out one of the secret tunnels?

Squeak!

Tally leapt back. Something red and furry wriggled from the stump of a tree. Popping out of a pile of leaves and soft moss was a baby squirrel. He stared up into her face, almost as though he'd been expecting her.

'Hello!' said Tally softly.

The squirrel blinked at her with wide black eyes. He was tiny, no bigger than Tally's hand. He rolled on to his back on the forest floor, with his four paws in the air and his red fur rippling as he shivered in the cold. Tally took her shawl from round her shoulders and tucked it over the squirrel.

'Here,' she said. 'That will warm you up.' She ignored the goosebumps that had sprung up on her bare arms.

The squirrel made a little chattering noise and buried himself in the wool.

'Wait there!' said Tally. 'I'll find you something to eat.' She dashed to the blackberry bushes and pulled off a juicy handful of berries.

'Eat up!' she said, holding out a fat blackberry. The squirrel cocked his head to the side, as if he was working out whether to trust Tally. Finally, he reached out a paw for the berry. It took him ages to eat such an enormous meal and, while he ate, Tally kept chatting to him.

'Have you lost your mum?' she asked. 'I've lost mine, too. Maybe they'll come back for us one day.

What do you think, Squill?' The squirrel stared
at her and took another nibble of his berry.
That was as much of an answer as she was going
to get.

The sun was beginning to rise and Tally could
see the forest much more clearly now. She turned
down her lamp and carried on looking for
firewood. Her pile of wood was slowly
growing. She jumped as a little paw added
a twig. The squirrel was helping her!

'Thank you, Squill,' she said.

The creature darted about in the undergrowth,
pulling up sticks. Then he leapt on to a low
branch and hung upside down by his back feet.

'That's very clever!' said Tally.
The squirrel gave an upside-down
shrug as if to say, *Well, hey, it's nothing
really.*

Tally smiled at him, at his fluffy
ears and his soft bushy tail. He was

her very first friend.

She opened her mouth to say something else, then hesitated.

Can I really ask a squirrel … ? Yes!

'Do … do … you want to come and live with me?' If she was very careful and if the squirrel managed to stay quiet, maybe she'd be able to sneak him past Mrs Sneed. It was a risk, but it was always so cold and lonely sleeping in that sink all on her own.

The squirrel gave her an upside-down stare. Then he swung upright on the tree branch and sat stroking his tail. Tally could tell he was thinking about it. She faltered. 'Or … maybe not … you don't have to …'

Suddenly Squill dived from the branch, landing softly on her shoulder. Tally laughed with relief as she felt his little paws squeeze her. 'Come on, then,' she said. 'I'll show you where you're going to sleep.'

CHAPTER THREE

Tally led the way across the forest, past the beehives, through the rose garden, across the cloisters, to the manor's side door. This door led to the servants' hallway, which was full of useful things like boots, logs for the fire, baskets of ribbons, brooms and mops. From there, a set of stairs led up to Lord Mollett's study. As Tally opened the side door she could hear loud voices: one bossy (that was Mr Bood), one spiky (that was Mrs Sneed) and one shrieky.

'It's Lady Mollett,' Tally whispered. 'Hide in my pinafore pocket, Squill! I want to hear what they are all saying.' The squirrel snuggled in.

Tally sneaked into the hallway, her arms filled with kindling. A group of people was gathered at the top of the stairs, outside Lord Mollett's study — where the burglary had taken place. As quietly as she could, Tally put the twigs into a basket on the tall dresser.

The dresser was slightly out of line — someone had pulled it away from the wall. It made the perfect hiding place! Tally squeezed behind it and strained her ears to hear what was going on.

'Our mother's ring. Gone!' Lady Mollett shrieked. 'Our father's watch. Vanished!' Tally peered out from behind the dresser to see Lady Mollett glancing from face to face, as if she was waiting for a reaction.

Lord Mollett had his eyes squeezed tight. 'My brooch, my bear,' he muttered, over and over again.

Lady Mollett flung the back of her hand against her forehead and slid to the floor.

'Fetch a glass of water, Tally,' Mrs Sneed called

down the stairs to her. It seemed that she wasn't so invisible, even hiding behind the dresser.

Tally slipped out and rushed to the kitchen.

'Wait here,' she whispered to Squill. She set him down in the pantry with a handful of nuts. Carrying a glass of water, she crept back into the hallway and up the stairs. Lady Mollett looked up from her pretend faint.

'Oh!' she cried, 'Who are you?'

Mrs Sneed gave Tally an icy look.

'This is my niece,' the housekeeper said quickly. 'Forget about her.' She waved a hand.

Tally stared hard at her feet. Broken glass from the cabinet door was strewn across the stone floor. Just by the cabinet, Tally noticed two sets of muddy footprints. One was a pattern of dots. *Those must be from hobnail boots,* Tally realised. Three dots were missing in the left middle. *The boot must be missing three nails.* The other set of prints was from a different

41

kind of boot. Tally leaned a little closer. *A riding boot?* She could see where the stirrup had worn a groove in the sole. No one in the manor house had shoes to match those prints. Tally did all the boot polishing, so she was sure of it. *These must be the burglars' footprints!*

Tally glanced back up. She had to tell everyone! But Mr Bood was shaking his head.

'There aren't any clues left behind,' he said. 'None at all!'

Tally cleared her throat loudly. Everyone looked at her.

'Um …' She pointed at the floor. 'There are footprints here,' she said. Mrs Sneed was frowning at her.

'By golly, yes!' said Lord Mollett. He knelt down and Mr Bood reluctantly followed, groaning at the effort of bending.

'It looks like the burglar stood here.' Mr Bood pointed to the hobnail print and frowned. 'Then I think he changed his shoes, and stepped here.'

What burglar would do that in the middle of a robbery?

'Or maybe …' Tally couldn't help herself.

Mrs Sneed drew a sharp breath. Lord Mollett didn't seem to notice. 'Go on,' he said. He had a kind face, soft round the edges.

'Oh Edward!' Lady Mollett cut in. 'We don't actually *talk* to the servants.'

Lord Mollett raised his eyebrows.

'What were you saying?' he said to Tally, after a pause.

Tally knew she'd get in trouble later but she was desperate to share her theory.

'I don't think there was one burglar who changed his shoes. I think there were two burglars. See!' She pointed again at the footprints. 'One in riding boots, one in hobnail boots. The sole of the riding boot is slightly worn down at the side …' Lord Mollett nodded, his eyes following the line of her finger. Tally took a deep breath and carried on

43

talking. 'And one of the hobnail boots is missing three nails here.'

'Tally, that's enough!' Mrs Sneed was furious. Lord Mollett shot a glance at the housekeeper. 'Er, I mean … thank you dear,' she added, softening her voice. 'Why don't you go downstairs and rest.' As Tally turned to leave, the housekeeper gave a final, fierce whisper: 'Peel the potatoes!'

Tally rushed down the stairs. From behind her, she heard Lord Mollett let out a cry.

'What ho! She's right!' Voices became muffled as the grown-ups bent over the footprints and Tally felt a little thrill of happiness. *Lord Mollett said I was right …*

That night Tally was sent to bed with no supper, but at least there was Squill's warm furry body to pat. Tally had set up his bed right next to her sink and it was wonderful to know he was there.

She raked her fingers through his soft fur and hummed a little song. It was a lullaby Ma used to sing to her at bedtime.

Give me your hand and we'll run
Down past the grass, up through the trees
Give me your time and we'll sail
Down to the boat, up on the seas
Give me your heart and we'll fly
Up like a bee, down under leaves
This is the answer I know
This is the truth I will see
All the way down I will go
Down where the gate waits for me.

Tally sang quietly.

Today had been a good day. She had met Squill. And Lord Mollett had praised her. He was the first person to be kind to her for years. Imagine if she solved the whole crime! Then he would smile at her and tell her how well she had done. She'd be the one who saved the manor. A warm feeling spread through her.

'Let's try to catch those burglars, Squill,' she said. She burrowed down deeper into her sink, putting Ma's scrap of lace under her cheek. With Squill by her side, anything felt possible.

Over the next few days, Tally's new friend grew more and more brave. Soon he was following her around the manor, chattering and dancing as she worked.

No one in the manor house noticed Squill. Everyone was far too busy setting traps to catch the burglars in case they came back. Lord Mollett's praise of Tally had not gone unnoticed and Sneed and Bood suddenly became determined not to be outdone by a scullery maid.

Mrs Sneed was designing a complicated scheme to catch the thief using a pair of barbecue tongs and a mousetrap. 'Tally!' she barked. 'Fetch me a fresh piece of cheese.'

Mr Bood planned to bash through the antique

marble floor with a sledgehammer, build a pit, cover it with leaves and trap the criminals when they fell in. 'Twooly!' he bossed. 'Fetch me a large bear.'

The other reason no one noticed Squill was because no one really noticed Tally, unless they were looking for someone to order about. The two friends could have gone for weeks and even months being overlooked, but Tally was about to make the most amazing discovery that meant that she'd never be invisible again.

On Friday morning, Tally was washing up in the kitchen. In her head she was running through ways the burglars might have got into the manor house. There was no sign that any doors or windows had been forced open, yet the criminals' footprints could clearly be seen leading through the hallway and up to the study. Maybe they *had* used a secret passage. There was one between the scullery and the infirmary, but it had a difficult entrance code and no footprints had been found anywhere near the infirmary door. Something tugged at her memory ... what was it? She was puzzling it through when Mr Bood came running in.

'A spider!' he squealed. Mr Bood was terrified of spiders (and snakes, and cauliflowers).

'Where?' cried Mrs Sneed, almost dropping her cup of tea.

'On the roses. The horrible six-legged beasts!'

Tally remembered Lord Mollett's reference book on spiders. She coughed. 'Um ... spiders have eight legs,' she said.

'Are you saying I can't count, Tolly?' Mr Bood boomed.

'Er, no.' She closed her mouth and washed another plate.

'And there were hundreds of those string thingies they make,' the butler continued.

'Webs?' Tally suggested, but the other two ignored her.

'We must clean the roses.
Right away!' Mrs Sneed
declared.

'Yes!' said Mr Bood. They both looked at
Tally. Tally sighed. She set the final plate on the
draining board and wiped her hands dry.

'Work hard, Tally!' called Mrs Sneed as Tally
picked up her cloth.

'Yes, Twilly,' added Mr Bood. 'Make sure you get
every one of those horrid insects!'

Tally was about to point out that spiders were
arachnids,[2] not insects, when she saw that Mr Bood
had sunk into a chair and was stuffing his face with
a large slice of chocolate cake. It looked like he'd
recovered from the shock.

In the rose garden, Tally gently lifted another stem.
Squill held the petal for her with his tiny paw, and
Tally delicately wiped it clean. She looked around.

[2] Arachnids have eight legs. They are invertebrate animals, which
means they don't have a spine. Insects have antennae, but arachnids
do not.

There were so many flowers! It was going to take hours to clean every petal. Tally sighed. She was desperate to go hunting for clues.

Tally didn't want to hurt any of the spiders so she and Squill carefully saved every one and put them in a box to take to the old stables. By the time the sun was high, Tally was exhausted and Squill was bored. He jumped behind the rose bushes and out again, silently begging Tally to play hide and seek. It was his favourite game.

'All right,' Tally agreed, 'but just one go. You hide while I take the spiders to the stables. They'll be safe there. Then we'll finish the roses and look for clues.'

Tally carefully placed the box of spiders down.

'There you go!' she said. 'I hope you'll be happy in your new home. There are lots of lovely dark dry corners to hide in.' She blew the spiders a kiss goodbye.

As she came out of the stables she spotted Squill

running into the forest. He was the best hider. He could curl up into a little ball and snuggle into tiny spaces. But despite this, Tally would still win every time as he could always be persuaded to come out for a ripe, fat blackberry.

This time, however, she didn't have any fruit. Tally wandered up and down in between the trees, looking carefully for a bit of red fluffy tail or a pair of black eyes. She had just passed a hollow tree when she heard Squill's mischievous giggle.

'Aha! Found you!' Tally cried, turning back.

Squill shrieked in excitement. He leapt out of the hollow and scampered through the forest.

'Slow down!' called Tally. 'I can't run that fast.'

She chased Squill through the trees right to the edge of the estate. Tally had never been this far from the manor house since Mrs Sneed had taken her in. She suddenly emerged from the woods to the scent of salt. Ahead of her, the cliffs met the sea. Goosepimples ran up Tally's arms as she looked around. *I remember this place.* This was where Ma had disappeared.

The edge of the cliff was cordoned off. A sign hung from the rope saying:

DANGER! NO ENTRY

'Squill!' Tally called. 'Where are you?' Her heart beat faster. She bit her lip to stem the rising feeling of panic. The wind was strong up here. It whistled past her ears like someone was calling. Had Ma cried out when she fell? Tally couldn't remember.

'Squill!' she shouted.

The only sound that came back was the roar of the sea.

CHAPTER FOUR

Tally peered over the cliff edge into the swirling water below. Her fingers rubbed at the bit of lace in her pocket.

'Squill!' Her voice grew more desperate. She spun around, away from the cliff, and her eyes swept over the grass, searching for a glimpse of his red fur.

There! She saw a small movement and four little legs scrambling. The squirrel was just to the left of her, by a group of giant stones. She ran to him and Squill jumped on to her shoulder. 'Don't ever leave me like that again,' she said, reaching up to stroke his fur. His whiskers trembled as if to say, *I'm sorry I scared you.*

Tally stepped back and gazed up at the old stones – there were five of them, four around the outside and one in the centre. Huge, ancient and mysterious, they towered over her, dark grey and mossy. Did the monks put them here, all those years ago? What were they for? Tally touched one and felt a shiver run up her spine. They felt funny … no … they felt … *familiar*. She'd been here before.

'Why did Ma bring me here that day?' She felt sure there was something important here. Something special. She walked slowly in between the stones, running her hand over each column. Her eyes were drawn to the largest stone in the centre of the group. As she came closer she saw that ten square holes were dotted around its base. An electric thrill shot through Tally. *Another puzzle!*

On the ground was a cube-shaped rock. She turned it over in her hands. Carved into one side of the cube was a shape. What did it remind her of? She peered closer. Oh! It was the image of a bee.

She put the cube into one of the holes in the huge central stone — it fit perfectly. *There must be more,* she thought. *Nine more.* Her eyes scanned the grass but she couldn't see any others.

'Squill, look at this.' Tally showed him the cube. 'We need to find more of these little rocks with pictures on them.' Quick as a flash Squill set to work, racing around the stone circle, picking up rocks and pebbles. He was super-fast.

'Found one,' cried Tally. This one had what looked like a heart on it. 'And another! How are you doing, Squill?' Squill waddled towards her with a pile of the cubes in his front paws. 'One, two, three, four, five, six, SEVEN! Well done, Squill,' Tally exclaimed. 'That's it. We've got all ten.'

Tally laid them all out on the grass to examine them. She couldn't work out all of the images, but she knew that the ten cubes must go into the ten holes in the great stone. One by one she began to put them in.

First, the bee,

then a hand,

a heart,

a boat,

a tree,

a long stalk,

something wiggly and wavy
(a snake, maybe?)

a funny hatching,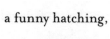

a leaf . . .

. . . until finally she came to the last one. It looked like a weirdly shaped woman. Slowly she leant forward, slotted it into the last remaining hole and waited.

Nothing.

Tally was not sure what she had been expecting, but she realised the monastery was not going to give up its secrets that easily. There must be some special order or arrangement. What could it be?

Tally was working out just how many arrangements there might be with ten cubes and ten holes[3] when Mrs Sneed's spiky voice rang out from a distance. 'Tally! Where are you, girl?'

Tally suddenly realised how far she was from the manor.

'Oh!' If anyone found out that she'd wandered this far away ... Tally gave a shudder and picked Squill up, placing him in her pocket. Together, they ran back through the forest and into the rose garden. Tally grabbed her duster and Squill dived behind a rose

---

[3] There are lots of different ways Tally can arrange the cubes in the holes. Each arrangement is called a permutation. Tally has 10 choices of where to put the first cube, then 9 remaining choices for the second cube, 8 for the third and so on. So she multiplies 10x9x8x7x6x5x4x3x2x1 to get over three and a half million possible permutations (3,628,800).

bush. They made it just as Mrs Sneed puffed into the rose garden, fists on her hips. The housekeeper strode over and inspected a rose stem. A tell-tale spider's web hung from a thorn and Mrs Sneed tutted loudly.

'Get on with it, girl!' she said, glancing around the garden. Her lips moved silently as she counted. 'You have fifty more bushes to clean before midday. Then I want you to sweep the cloister and clean the tapestry corridor. After that I need you to find the right cheese for my burglar trap.'

Tally could see Squill just behind Mrs Sneed. He was stretching his neck out long and thin and waggling his paw in a perfect imitation of the housekeeper. Tally smothered a giggle and bent her head over a rose bush until Mrs Sneed had gone.

'That was close,' Tally whispered to Squill. He cracked his neck in response.

For the rest of the day the cubes haunted Tally's thoughts. What were they? As she swept the cloister she puzzled it through. She'd always felt Mollett

Manor was magic, as though it was trying to tell her something. What were those symbols on the cubes? What did they mean?

Tally headed through the side door into the servants' hallway. She stopped by the large wooden dresser. It had been pushed back in place now but something caught Tally's eye. There on the wall, snagged on the rough stone, was a scrap of fluffy wool. Tally pulled it away. It was bright red. She'd never seen anyone at the manor with a jumper or scarf of that colour.

'It's a clue, Squill!' she whispered and she put the wool into her pinafore pocket.

Tally carried her dustpan and broom into the tapestry corridor. The flagstoned hallway was filled with large vases, embroidered tapestries and empty suits of armour. She leaned her broom against the wall. Squill balanced on the tip of the broomstick and swept the walls with his tail while Tally dusted the tapestries.

Her favourite tapestry was the one by the door to
the ballroom. It was the oldest and most worn and
it had been at the manor since the time when the
house had been a monastery.

Tally loved the ancient wall-hanging. It was an
embroidery of a garden full of animals and flowers,
trees, birds and bees, and in the background was
the sea. To the far left five monks stood in a group
wearing long dark-grey habits.[4]

Sometimes, when the lonely nights seemed
endless, Tally would sneak up to the tapestry

[4] A habit is a long hooded outfit worn by monks.

corridor. By the moonlight she'd gaze at all the different images, marvelling at the criss-cross of threads and thinking of all the people who must have spent hours of their lives embroidering it. Every time she looked at the tapestry she noticed something new.

'Do you like it, Squill?' Tally whispered and Squill nodded. He jumped on her shoulder to examine an image of a hazelnut. 'Looking at this has got me through some hard times.' Tally stroked the bottom of the tapestry. It was like an old friend.

But looking at it today, something felt different. She took a step back. What did those monks remind her of?

Of course, the five monks, covered in grey, looked just like the five stones near the cliff! One of the monks was waving with his hand. *A hand ...*

'That's one of the images on the cubed rocks!' Tally cried.

Could this tapestry be some kind of clue to the puzzle? She took another step back to take in the whole scene. What were the other images on the

cubes? Were they in the tapestry

too? She ran her eyes over the

embroidery and saw: bees by the

hive in the top right, a

boat on the river in the

foreground

and a group of

trees on the left.

Tally began to breathe a

little faster.

What about the snakey thing? Tally searched

and searched, and while she was looking

for the snake she noticed: long stalks

of grass, a pile

of leaves and a

 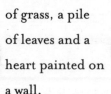

heart painted on

a wall.

But there was no snake anywhere to be

seen. *What else could that wavy line be?* Tally searched for it.

She tried to remember what the snake-shaped carving had looked like. She closed her eyes. It had been a single wavy line. Of course, it was the waves on the sea!

What was left? Squill leapt on to her head, bringing his nose close to the hanging. He chewed the end of Tally's hair to help her think.

The weird wiggly woman ... Tally examined the tapestry again. She couldn't see the woman anywhere. To the right of the monks was a funny-shaped log. It looked a bit like the woman. Tally brought her face so close that all the images began to blur together. She screwed up her eyes and then snapped them open. The shape wasn't a log or a woman, either. It was an hourglass! Now there was just one remaining image to find. That odd little cube with the hatching on it. *No, not hatching ...*

'Squill,' breathed Tally. 'A gate. It was a gate!' She pointed. There, on the tapestry, leading out of the garden on the bottom-right corner, was a tiny gate picked out in brown silk thread.

'It's a pattern,' she said to Squill. 'The tapestry is a map to the position of the cubes. It's telling me which holes to put them in.'

I need to remember where each one is, she thought, and closing her eyes she began to imagine herself in front of the great stone. 'Hand, grass, tree,' she murmured to fix them in her head.

'We have to go back to the stones,' she whispered to Squill. 'Tonight.'

When everyone was tucked up in bed, Tally climbed out of her sink and tiptoed with Squill to the back of the scullery. There was a secret passageway here she had discovered years ago. Over the fireplace was a stone archway. It had a phrase carved into its ancient curve:

EXPERTS SNOOP

Tally had worked out that rearranging these letters gave: **PRESS X TO OPEN.**

She pressed on the letter 'X' and there was a low groan as the stone wall behind the fireplace creaked open to reveal a set of steps leading down to a dark corridor.

'This way, Squill,' whispered Tally. She held the lamp above her head so they could see. He sniffed and sneezed.

'I know. Smells a bit musty.' Tally nodded at him. 'Don't worry. It goes straight out to the old infirmary. You'll see!' Together they walked through the dark tunnel. Tally knew her way quite well.

'Here!' she cried as they reached the end. Tally turned a handle and leant her weight against the stone door. It creaked open to reveal a sliver of light and they stepped out into the infirmary fireplace.

'Quick!' Tally rushed across the old hospital and out of the back door. Holding the lamp up high, she sped past the beehives, round the back of the malthouse, through the woods and all the way to the stone circle.

Tally pulled the cubes out of the holes where she had left them and laid them on the ground next to the lamp. She pursed her lips, trying to remember the pattern from the tapestry. She was sure of the first three. *The hand was here in the far left where the monks stood,* she thought as she placed it in the stone, *then it was down to the grass and up to the tree.*

'Down past the grass, up to the tree,' she muttered to herself. Tally suddenly stopped – that was a line from Ma's lullaby.

'Squill!' Her voice shook. She sang the whole line: '*Give me your hand and we'll run, down past the grass, up through the trees*. Oh!' A flood of warmth swept over Tally. 'Ma knew! She knew about the cubes with the symbols! She must have solved this puzzle as well. The lullaby could have been her way of remembering the pattern.'

Tally grinned as she put the cubes in. Squill

jumped up and down on his back paws.

'Give me your time and we'll sail, down to the boat, up on the seas.' Tally paused. 'Time! The hourglass would represent time! So that goes here in the middle and then the boat down here, and the wavy line up there.'

With the lullaby in her head it was as if Ma was with her, guiding her towards solving the puzzle.

'Give me your heart and we'll fly, up like a bee, down under leaves.' Quickly Tally placed the heart cube in the hole, the bee above and the leaf below.

Now there was only one cube remaining and one hole. The gate, just where it had been on the tapestry, in the bottom-right corner leading out and away. How did Ma's lullaby end?

> This is the answer I know
> This is the truth I will see
> All the way down I will go
> Down where the gate waits for me.

What would happen when she placed the final
cube?

Tally hesitated, rolling the cube around between
her fingers.

'This is the last piece, Squill. Let's do it together.'

Squill jumped up and reached out a paw to help
Tally put it in its place.

Crunch!

The two of them leapt back from the stone. Tally
looked at Squill, Squill looked at Tally. The ancient
stone began to shudder and shake. Then the
shuddering stopped. She heard a long squeak, like
rusty knives being sharpened. Except it wasn't. By
Tally's feet, a trapdoor was opening in the grass!

CHAPTER FIVE

Tally knelt down to peer into the opening. She
thrust her hands into the dark space and her fingers
closed around ... rope and wood.

'It's a rope ladder, Squill!' she cried. A shiver
ran down Tally's spine. 'You hold the lamp.' Squill
wrapped his little arms around the base. 'Now climb
on my back. Hold on tight.' The squirrel scrambled
on to her back, clutching the lamp with one paw.
Then Tally turned herself around and carefully
reached out a foot for the start of the ladder. The
rope creaked with her weight and the ladder swung
from side to side, but she clung on.

Step by step, Tally climbed down into the hole. Her heart was thumping wildly.

'Mr Bood wouldn't like it here, Squill,' she said, trying to make her voice sound brave as the trapdoor squeaked closed above her. 'There are cobwebs everywhere.'

The squirrel squeezed his paws into her shoulder to give her courage.

It was damp and musty and it smelt like dogs rolling around in puddles, but they kept going down until eventually the ladder stopped. Tally reached out a foot and felt solid ground. She stepped off the ladder and took the lamp from Squill.

They were in an enormous underground room. The air felt sharp, electrified.

Trembling, she lifted the lamp higher, and gasped.

Books. There were hundreds of books.

She cried out in joy.

A library!

An underground library!

It was filled with the books from her dreams. How had she known they would be here?

'Ma,' she whispered. It was to do with Ma, she was sure. Had her mum told her? Her forehead creased as she tried to remember. Mr Bear had come here in a story, wearing one of his hats.

'This must be why she brought me to the cliffs that day,' she murmured. 'To show me how to find this place.' She looked at the squirrel. 'Thank you, Squill. You brought me back to the giant stones.'

There were lamps dotted around the room. With a shaking hand, Tally pulled a box of matches out of her pinafore pocket and lit the lamps one by one. A glow filled the room.

This was no
ordinary library.
There were no
aisles and neat ordered
rows. Here shelves
twisted and turned and
corkscrewed from floor to ceiling.
No shelf was level — each seemed to curve into the
next so Tally could hardly tell where one shelf ended
and another began. She looked up and the ceiling
narrowed to a tiny point high, high above her. Here
and there were little wobbly ladders which stretched
up to reach the highest levels.

The shelves were crammed with books of all
shapes and sizes and colours. Some were bound in
leather, some in gold. Some were tied with fading
ribbon, some with a kind of twine. Their edges
were worn and their spines cracked as if they'd been
thumbed over and over again through the ages.

'Oh, Squill!' Tally clapped her hands. Her

dreams had come true!

She chose a book and blew the dust away to reveal a heavy leather-bound cover. It was very old. Tally could feel its spine was wrinkled and crumbly beneath her fingers.

THE MAP BOOK OF ATLANTIS, she read. Her eyes widened.

She chose another. **DESIGNS FOR STONEHENGE.**

And another. **THE SECOND BOOK OF IRISH DANCING: HOW TO USE THE ARMS.**

'Wow, Squill. These are lost books! Secret books! Look: **BASIC ALCHEMY**. That's how to make gold.' She began to pull down more and more books, faster and faster. **'THE DIARY OF BIGFOOT, HOW TO FIND LOST SOCKS, THE SECRET TO YOUNGER-LOOKING SKIN, THE SQUIRREL MAP OF BURIED NUTS!'**

Squill pricked up his ears.

Tally could hardly speak.

'Imagine, Squill,' said Tally. 'All these secret books here for centuries!'

Her fingers ran *bump, bump, bump* along the dusty spines. She chose a book at random.

SPIDER BEHAVIOUR by Paddy Long Legs.

'Oh, Lord Mollett would love this book!' She sat down in a corner to open it. 'This chapter's called "Spiderlings", Squill. It's about spider babies!'

Tally began to read out loud.

'Some female spiders can lay over one thousand eggs. The eggs are sticky and they glue themselves together.'

As Tally's voice echoed off the stone walls the strangest thing happened. She'd always had a good imagination, and she'd always been able to picture the characters or place in a story. But now, it was as though the spiders were really with her. They scuttled around in front of her on the dusty floor.

Tally could see their markings clearly, and hear the rustle of their feet. She leapt up in shock. The book slammed closed and the spiders disappeared.

'Did you see them?' She could hear her
voice shaking. The squirrel nodded and waggled his
red tail.

Tally sat back down. She breathed in and out
slowly. With trembling fingers she picked the book
up. Gathering her courage, she began to read out
loud again.

*'The mother spider builds a silken egg sac to protect her
babies.'*[5]

Tally's mouth dropped open as the
spiders reappeared. They danced before her
eyes, making a bed of silk in mid-air and
wrapping up their balls of eggs tightly. Tally hardly
dared breathe as she watched them. They looked
so real! She reached out and gingerly
poked a spider. Her finger slipped straight
through the image.

'It's some kind of hologram, Squill,' she
whispered. The squirrel nodded wisely, as if he

[5] The wolf spider carries the egg sac everywhere she goes. When the
babies hatch they ride on her back until they are big enough to fend
for themselves.

knew what the word 'hologram'[6] meant.

Tally continued reading.

'After the eggs hatch, the spiderlings cut their way out of the silk sac,' Tally read. 'Look, Squill. They're so cute!'

Tiny baby spiders were rushing out of the fluffy white sac. They were brown and blotchy and they ran about in circles. Then they pointed their spinnerets[7] into the air.

'The wind pulls a thread of silk from the baby spider's spinneret. The thread lifts the baby and the spiderling floats on the breeze, pulled by the thread for miles and miles.'

The tiny spiders were drifting through the sky. The air was cool and fresh and Tally could feel the sun on her back as the spiders floated along. 'Goodbye!' She waved as they drifted away.

Tally closed the book and gazed at Squill.

'Do you know what this means?' she asked her closest friend in the world. The squirrel shrugged his shoulders as though to say, *No, but you're going to tell me anyway.* Tally laughed and picked

[6] A hologram is a three-dimensional (3D) image.
[7] A spinneret is the silk-spinning organ of the spider.

Squill up to hug him tightly. 'The books are magic,'
she said, as she gazed around the Secret Library.
'They're magic, Squill!'

CHAPTER SIX

Tally could barely take in everything that had
happened.

A thread of wonder tingled through her body.
With these books she could find out anything she
wanted to know, and see anything she wanted to see.
She thought about Lord Mollett and the thieves.
Now she was certain to solve the crime! A smile
spread across her face, stretching from ear to ear.

'Let's explore!' she cried, jumping up.

Together, she and Squill ran further into the
library. They sped past:

ANIMALS (Aardvark to Zebra)

CHEMICALS (Acetone to Zirconium)

HORTICULTURE (Acacia to Zinnia)

LANGUAGES (Arabic to Zulu)

MUSIC (Accordion to Zither)

PHILOSOPHY (Aristotle to Zeno)

SPORT (Archery to Ziplining)

WEATHER (Air pressure to Zonal flow)

ZOOLOGY (Animal psychology to Zoography)

. . . on and on and round and round and back to the start again until they were exhausted.

With all the lamps lit, the library was filled with a soft glow, making the gold lettering sparkle on the book spines. Something on the wall caught Tally's attention. She picked up her lamp and moved closer.

At the entrance, just by the rope ladder, Tally could see letters carved into the stone wall.

'*Welcome, Secret Keeper,*' Tally read. 'Secret Keeper?' she repeated, glancing at Squill quickly.

'*You have found the library of the Minervian Monks,*' Tally read on. '*We began this library in the year 1150 to preserve our knowledge and protect the information we discovered.*'

'Wow, Squill!' cried Tally. 'The library is hundreds of years old. It says: *In 1250 there was a disaster. A wicked man tried to use our knowledge for evil. Many people died. The library entrance was sealed to everyone except the Secret Keeper.*'

Below the introduction was a scroll, pinned to the wall with nails.

The Secret Library's Rules:

There will be only one Secret Keeper
in each generation.

The Secret Keeper must be
under the age of thirteen.

The Keeper must guard the secret of
the library and the information within.

Talking is permitted.

Tally's legs felt like jelly. She slid down to sit on the dusty ground.

'I think I'm the Secret Keeper,' she said.

Squill nodded wisely.

Tally took a deep breath.

'I have this library for three years,' she said, 'until I'm thirteen.' She folded her arms. 'Squill, we have a lot of learning to do!'

In the far distance, she heard the church bell ring out from the local village. It struck four times. In an hour from now, at five in the morning, Mrs Sneed would be dragging Tally out of the kitchen sink to start lighting the fires. But if Tally wasn't there …

She leapt to her feet.

'Come on, Squill. Time to get back!'

The squirrel scrambled on to Tally's back and they ran through the library.

Hand over hand, she climbed the rope ladder as fast as she could. At the top, she felt around for a catch to open the trapdoor. Her fingers closed around a little lever in a hollow of stone. She pulled hard and the trapdoor creaked open. Tally and Squill were suddenly bathed in moonlight. They clambered up, removed the cubes from their holes and watched as the trapdoor sealed itself again.

'I'm going to put the cubes back in the wrong order, Squill,' said Tally, moving them around. 'Now I'm a Secret Keeper I have to protect the library.'

With Squill bouncing in her pinafore pocket, Tally ran through the woods, past the malthouse and the beehives to the old infirmary. The infirmary's fireplace matched the one in the scullery, so Tally pressed the 'X' in EXPERTS SNOOP and rushed down the musty tunnel.

They were halfway along the tunnel when they heard a loud crash and tinkle of glass. Tally froze.

'Look what you's done now, Joe!' came a muffled voice.

Tally frowned. She recognised every voice at the

manor and that didn't sound like anyone she knew.

'It's the burglars,' Tally whispered to Squill.

'You said we's get the sofa,' a voice answered. 'You said!'

'It's not on the plan. Look!'

'I don't care about the plan, Harry!'

Tally heard a ripping sound, like paper being torn up.

'Stop that, Joe. We needs the plan. Come on. We's got to go!'

Tally could just hear the sound of footsteps fading as the burglars ran out towards the garden. She rushed back down the tunnel and pressed the inside catch of the passage as quickly as she could. But, by the time she burst out into the manor grounds, the burglars had gone. The sun was rising and Tally could make out their muddy prints in the soft ground. A hobnail boot with three missing nails, and a pair of riding boots. The tracks led through the woods to a hole in the high garden wall. *So that's how the burglars are getting into the manor grounds.*

But there was something puzzling Tally. In the tunnel, when she'd heard the burglars, the sounds hadn't come from ahead, from inside the manor house. They had come from the *side*, from someone at the same level as Tally.

'There must be another tunnel, Squill.' Tally ran through the layout of the house. Where was the tunnel entrance? She walked back through the woods and stopped when she reached the garden. To her right was the infirmary. To her left was the old malthouse. Nowadays it was filled with junk. Old lawnmowers that didn't work, broken gardening tools, rusty paint tins. No one ever went in there. Could there be a tunnel leading from it?

The village bell rang five times. There was no time to find out.

'Mrs Sneed! Quick, Squill. We have to be inside before she gets up!'

*　*　*

They made it back to the sink just in time. Tally gulped in great gasps of air as Squill hid down in her pinafore pocket. The housekeeper's spiky footsteps rang out on the tiles as she walked from her room through the kitchen to the scullery.

'I see you are up,' she said, her face falling.

'I heard a noise,' Tally said quickly. 'I think it was the burglars!'

Mrs Sneed glanced around nervously. 'Well, what are you waiting for?' she snapped. 'Go and see. I'll be right behind you.' Mrs Sneed put the kettle on the hob. 'About twenty minutes behind you.'

For once Tally didn't mind Mrs Sneed's laziness. This way, she could look for clues. She walked through the kitchen to the servants' hallway. The wooden dresser against the wall was out of place again.

'Hmm,' said Tally.

There were muddy footprints on the floor. Her heart skipped a beat when she saw where they led.

Down the tapestry corridor! Surely the burglars hadn't taken the precious garden tapestry? Her heartbeat quickened as she peered down the corridor. *Phew.* The tapestry was still there.

The ballroom door was ajar. Tally pushed it open with a feeling of dread.

The large chandelier was gone! It usually hung in the centre of the room, sparkling with hundreds of crystals. The burglars had taken the beautiful ornament. Now, in the middle of the room, there was nothing but a stepladder. Squill jumped out of her pocket and began hunting for clues.

'Tally?'

'In here, Mrs Sneed,' Tally called back. She waved at Squill to hide behind the sofa.

'What have you done with the chandelier?' The housekeeper gazed around the ballroom.

'It wasn't me!' Tally protested. 'The burglars took it.'

'I need to search you,' the housekeeper snapped.

Tally lifted her arms up in confusion. Did Mrs Sneed expect to find a chandelier in her pinafore pocket?

'What's this?' Mrs Sneed's voice was icy.

Tally looked down in a panic. Had she accidentally brought a book from the Secret Library? To her relief Mrs Sneed was holding an acorn from the forest. Squill had picked a whole stash yesterday.

'Are you stealing food, Tally?' Mrs Sneed continued.

'Er … um … no … it's just an acorn.'

'Corn?' Mrs Sneed looked suspicious.

'No: *aaa*corn.' Tally stressed the first part of the word. 'It contains the seed of an oak tree.'

Mrs Sneed raised her eyebrows. 'No growing trees in the scullery,'

the housekeeper said finally. 'You need to be getting on with your chores.'

'Yes, Mrs Sneed.' Tally hesitated for a moment. Here was her chance to really help. Maybe she could show everyone that she could do more than just chores. Tally took a deep breath. 'Do you want me to look for clues? I could help. I mean ...' She began to falter under the housekeeper's gaze.

'No,' Mrs Sneed said firmly.

'I could be useful.'

Mrs Sneed snorted. 'Sadly, you are no use at all. Go to Lord Mollett's room and tell him about the chandelier.' Mrs Sneed sat herself down on the ballroom sofa. 'He doesn't like being woken up so I'm not going to do it.'

'Yes, Mrs Sneed.'

Lord Mollett wasn't in his room. Tally decided to try his study. The door was half open and she was just about to knock when she heard a loud sob. Tally held her breath. Lord Mollett was sitting at his desk with his head in his hands.

'My brooch,' he was mumbling through his tears. 'My bear.'

Tally shrank back. She gave a cough and stamped her feet as if she was coming up the stairs. Then she knocked on the door.

She heard Lord Mollett clear his throat. 'Come in,' he called. He smiled when he saw Tally. 'Hello! It's Tally, isn't it? Mrs Sneed's niece?'

Tally took a deep breath. She wasn't Mrs Sneed's niece — she didn't have any family. But Mrs Sneed would be furious if Tally told the truth.

'Mrs Sneed wanted me to tell you that there's been another burglary,' she said. 'Thieves have stolen the ballroom chandelier.'

'Oh no!' he cried. 'We have to catch those burglars.'

He thumped a fist into the palm of his hand. He looked at Tally and his face lit up. 'You're a clever girl. Do you have any ideas?'

'Me?' Tally faltered. No one at the manor had ever asked to hear her thoughts before.

'Yes,' said Lord Mollett. 'You're the most sensible person we have around here.'

Tally blushed. A warm feeling spread across her.

The lord glanced down at his empty hands. 'Some of those items the burglars took … They were very precious to me.'

Tally nodded. 'I liked that brooch too,' she said.

'It's lovely, isn't it? Someone special made it for me.' He stood up. 'Come on. Let's take a look at the damage in the ballroom.'

Tally couldn't stop grinning as she followed him down the stairs. Lord Mollett thought she was clever. Clever and sensible! She was more determined than ever to find those burglars.

'The Secret Library can help us, Squill,' she whispered. There was an answering wriggle of excitement from her pocket.

CHAPTER SEVEN

Tally rushed through her chores, ironing sheets, dusting mantelpieces and polishing floors at top speed. By lunchtime her arms were exhausted, but she was finished.

She knew what she wanted to investigate first: the wooden dresser. Twice she'd seen it pushed out from the wall. Plus, this was where she'd found the scrap of red wool.

In the servants' hallway she checked for Sneed and Bood before slipping behind the large dresser. She crept along, brushing her hands along the wall. About halfway, she found a crack. Tally lifted her lamp to inspect it. There was a door in the wall! She fumbled to try to find a code but, to her surprise, the door didn't need one. It swung open to reveal a sloping path leading underground. She'd never seen this passage before!

'Watch out for clues,' she told her friend.

The squirrel chattered and jumped from her shoulder down to the ground.

Together they combed the tunnel, checking the walls and the floor. It took ages and Tally kept sneezing from the dust. At last, Squill gave a squeal of triumph.

'What is it, Squill?'

Halfway down the passage, there were pieces of glass on the floor. Tally shone her lamp over the prisms. They reflected the light, sending the soft glow bouncing around the tunnel.

'It's glass from the chandelier!' Tally cried.

She searched the ground. There, next to the glass, was a pile of ripped-up paper. Tally lifted a small piece and smoothed it out. On it was written:

Steal chandelier.

'This is the plan the burglars were arguing about!' Tally cried. Together they gathered up all the bits of paper and Tally put them in her pocket.

'We'll stick them together,' she said. 'But first, I want to see where this tunnel leads.'

The path sloped up. At the end was a stone door. Caught on a tiny chip was a thread of red wool.

'The burglars definitely came this way!'

Tally pushed the door open. They were in the malthouse junk room! Suddenly she realised why the tunnel didn't have a code.

'In Lord Mollett's book about the history of the manor, it said the monks brewed their ale in here and transported it straight to the refectory — our kitchen. They must have used this tunnel all the time. It wasn't a secret passage, so it didn't need a code!' Squill nodded wisely. 'I guess, when it wasn't used anymore, the dresser was just put in front of the door and everyone forgot about it. But we found it! And now we know how the burglars are getting in and out.' She looked at Squill. 'I should have known those burglars were too silly to find their way through a secret passageway. Right. Let's have a look at this paper.'

Tally pushed aside an old rocking chair with a missing base and swept the floor clean with a rag from her pocket. She tipped out the torn scraps and bent over them, moving the pieces round and round to fit them together like a jigsaw. Finally, she had a note. It read:

SNATCH 'N' GRAB BURGLARS INC.

MISSION STATEMENT: To steal stuff

COMPANY MOTTO: What you seize is what you get

PLAN: Take small things from Mollett Manor
so we're not discovered.
PLUS A SOFA

SCHEDULE:

MONDAY – Break into Mollett Manor.
Steal jewellery. *AND A SOFA*

TUESDAY – Do laundry.

WEDNESDAY – Yoga night.

THURSDAY – Feed next door's cat.

FRIDAY – Break into Mollett Manor.
Steal chandelier.

DON'T FORGET SOFA

Stop goin on about a sofa Joe – we's not takin one

BUT I NEEDS ONE

SATURDAY – Break into Mollett Manor.
Steal valuable tapestry. AND A SOFA

ROUTE:

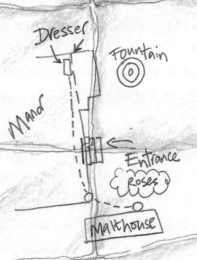

HEALTH AND SAFETY
ASSESSMENT:

Tunnel is v dark – bring torch.
Mum says wrap up warm.

'Squill!' Tally cried. 'It's Saturday. Those burglars are coming back tonight. And they're planning to steal the old tapestry!'

Squill chattered crossly.

'We can't let them take it.' Tally's eyes filled with tears. The wall-hanging had always been precious but, now that she knew it held the secret symbols, the symbols in Ma's lullaby, it was more special to her than ever. 'We have to stop them.' She stood up quickly. Squill paced around her in a circle. 'We need to catch them. That way we can force them to give us back Lord Mollett's brooch and bear, too. And the chandelier. Let's go to the Secret Library,' said Tally. 'There's bound to be something about catching things in the books there.'

The wind whipped around the cliff top. Tally sat in the centre of the stones and placed the cubes in the right pattern. As she put the last cube in place — the one with

the gate symbol – the trapdoor creaked
open. Tally grinned at Squill and they made
their way down, down, down the rope ladder under the
ground and into the Secret Library.

Tally couldn't stop smiling as she looked at all
the books. She settled down in the animals section
(Aardvark to Zebra).

'What about **TRACKING ANIMALS by Ivor Cent**?'

Squill shook his head.

'Um … **ANIMAL TRAPS by A.M. Bush**?'

Squill nodded. He was right – this might be just the
book to help them trap burglars. Tally pulled down a
dark leather book and placed it on the floor in front
of her. She looked at Squill and Squill looked at her.
They were both remembering how the spiders had
come out the last time she'd opened a book.

'OK.' Her voice was shaking a little. 'Here goes …'

She opened the cover and found the contents
page. It listed all kinds of different animals who
made traps to catch prey.

Chapter 3 (pages 34–36) was about the snapping turtle. Nervously, Tally turned to page 34 and started to read:

'*The common snapping turtle is a freshwater turtle found in Canada.*'

As she read, a large turtle rose out of the book. It was the size of a dinner plate and it swam round and round in the air above her. It had a large beak-like mouth and sharp claws. There was a loud smack as it opened its strong jaws and snapped them shut. Tally drew back, but the hologram paid them no attention, and just carried on swimming around. Tally read on:

'*To catch its prey, the turtle camouflages itself as a rock.*'

At this, the turtle landed on the floor and pulled its head and legs into its shell.

'Oh yes, it looks just like a rock!' cried Tally. 'Hmm. I'm not sure we could camouflage ourselves very well against the hallway wall. Besides, what would we do when the burglars came in?'

She turned back to the index and all at once the

snapping turtle disappeared.

'Let's try chapter six, Squill,' said Tally. 'It's all about the Venus flytrap. *The Venus flytrap is a carnivorous plant,*[8] she read out.

All at once a lime-green stalk pushed its way through the pages of the book, followed by four more. At the end of each stalk was a leaf in the shape of a clam shell. Tally continued reading.

'The inside of the leaf is red, making it look like a flower.'

One of the leaves obediently opened for Tally and Squill to see inside. It was a deep pinky-red, and around its edges was a row of long hairs.

'Those hairs are called guard hairs,' said Tally,

---

[8] This means it eats meat.

skimming the page. *'Inside the leaf there are trigger hairs. When a fly lands on a hair twice in a row, the leaf snaps shut.'* The leaf closed to demonstrate.

'A giant Venus flytrap would be useful! We could catch the burglars in it ... only ... wait ... oh no ... it says here that the plant catches the fly to eat it.'

As a fly buzzed towards the plant, Tally quickly slammed the book shut before the leaf could trap it.

'Ew. We don't want the burglars *eaten*!'

Squill gave a little chatter and held out something in his paw.

'What's that you've got there, Squill? A cobweb?'

The squirrel gently placed it on her hand. It felt soft and sticky.

'Oh, I see! We could make a spider web.'

Squill nodded his furry head.

'That's perfect! It will trap them without hurting them. Now there must be a book about webs somewhere here ...' She climbed one of the ladders to get a closer look at the higher shelves. The books up here were really dusty. Squill scampered beside her and brushed the spines with his tail, puffing little clouds of dust across the library.

Tally ran her eyes over the books. One had a low glow about it, making it shine out against the others. A prickle of excitement ran down Tally's spine. She read the title out loud:

'THE SECRETS OF SPIDER WEBS by S. Ticky.'

With trembling fingers, Tally pulled the book from the shelf and climbed back down the ladder.

As she opened the cover the old spine cracked softly. A low humming noise came from the pages. Tally looked at Squill. There was something extra special about this book.

At the beginning was an introduction, written in green ink in old crooked writing. It said:

**For centuries scientists have been trying
to make spider silk.[9] But no one knows how
to reproduce the sticky, stretchy thread.
This book will tell you how. But you
must promise never to give the secret away.**

Tally lifted her finger to turn the page, but, to her surprise, the pages were stuck fast together. She frowned. She read the last line again.

You must promise never to give the secret away.

'I promise,' she whispered.

The book gave a soft sigh, and the pages flipped open. Tally sat back on her heels and began to read.

'In equal diameter spider silk is five times stronger than steel.'

Squill tilted his head to the side.

'I think that means that if you took a thread of steel and a thread of spider silk the same thickness, the spider silk would be five times stronger. Wow, that's really strong.'

She turned back to the book.

[9] This thread could be very useful in packaging, in sailing and even in the army.

'Spider silk is made of a protein called fibroin. Proteins!' said Tally. 'I've read about those before in one of Lord Mollett's books.'[10]

The book turned its own page and Tally gave a little shiver.

'Spiders have spinnerets in the lower part of their abdomen.'

At this, a spider floated up out of the book and rolled over gracefully to show Tally her tummy. There, at the base, were six little bumps.

'I think those are the spinnerets,' Tally whispered.

As they watched, thin threads began to come out of the spinnerets. They twisted together and became one long thread. Then the spider began to spin.

First, she licked all eight of her legs so they wouldn't stick to her own web. She ran round and round in a circle to create the centre of the web. Tally watched as the web grew bigger and bigger. Soon a beautiful shape shone before her, sparkling in the lamplight. The book turned a page and, instantly, both the spider and the web disappeared.

[10] Proteins are the building blocks of all living things. They help your body make and repair cells.

'*How to make spider silk.*' Tally read the title of the next page and grinned at Squill. 'Now we can make a web and catch those burglars.'

There was a long list of ingredients. To reproduce the spider silk she had to find celery and pasta and potatoes and leeks and chicken bones and flour and hair from her hairbrush. She nodded as she read, then stopped as she came to the final ingredient: spider essence.

'What's that?' But Squill didn't know either.

Tally's eyes flicked down the page. '*The secret of silk belongs to the spiders. If you wish to know it, you must ask permission.*'

Tally kept reading. She knew the book would tell her what to do next ...

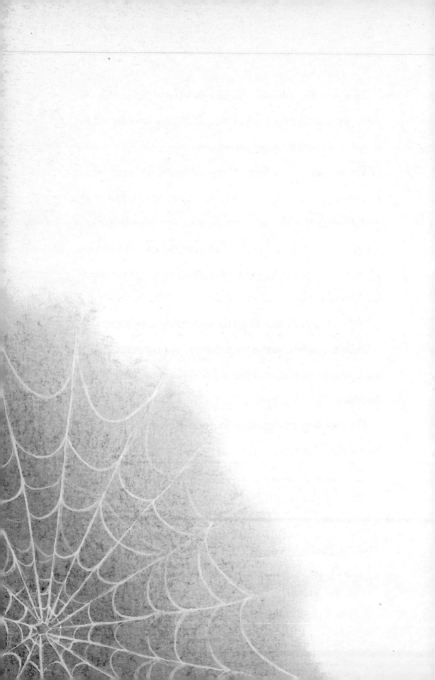

CHAPTER EIGHT

Tally pushed open the creaky door to the old stables. Right at the back was the box she had brought here days earlier, full of the spiders she'd rescued from the rose petals. She hoped the spiders remembered her, because she needed their help now.

But the box was empty. Where were all the spiders? Then she looked up. Hanging from the rafters of the building were hundreds of webs.

The magic book had given Tally a phrase to say. She'd practised it over and over until she knew it perfectly. She shuffled her feet and looked at Squill. Then she pulled back her shoulders and addressed the webs:

'Spider, spider
My heart is true
Help me learn
To do what you do.'

Tally placed a little bowl on the floor. If all went well, the spiders would fill this with their special spider essence.

'I hope that works!' Tally whispered to Squill.

They hid in the shadows of the stables.

Before long the webs began to twitch. A long thin thread twirled from a cobweb just above them. It was a spider dropping down! Tally held her breath and the little spider scampered to the bowl. Moments later it was gone, back up the thread again to its web. Tally watched in amazement as spider after spider hung down to the bowl, and climbed back up again.

Tally took a nervous step forward and lifted the bowl. It was filled with a silver gel! She crouched down and gently touched it with her finger. It was light but sticky and she rubbed it between her finger and thumb, feeling its stretchiness. Her heart gave a little extra beat of happiness.

'Thank you!' she cried to the spiders.

The village bell struck six. Not long till night time. They would set the trap as soon as everyone had gone to bed. Tally felt a bubble of excitement swelling in her tummy. But first, there were a few more ingredients to collect …

'There you are!' snapped Mrs Sneed as Tally appeared in the kitchen. 'These vegetables need peeling for dinner. Hurry up or you'll never get it done!' Then she cut herself a large piece of cake and headed off for a nice sit-down.

As Tally peeled and chopped, Squill sneaked away some of the celery, potatoes and leeks to use in the magic spider silk recipe. He had made a hiding place under the scullery floor by moving an old stone and he buried the vegetables quickly, his little paws moving so fast they were a blur.

'Well done!' said Tally. 'We still need some flour, chicken bones, pasta and some hair. Do you think you can find all that?'

Squill stood to attention and saluted. Then he scampered off to track everything down. Tally smiled as she watched him. She could hardly remember life without her friend.

Late that night, while everyone slept, Tally and
Squill heaved a large pot on to the stove.
Into it they added:
Leeks,
potatoes,
celery,
hair,
pasta,
chicken bones and
flour.

114

They moved as quietly as possible. Every now and then Squill disappeared down the corridor to check that Mr Bood was still snoring.

Tally stirred and stirred.

Round and round she mixed, until the stew became gloopier and thicker.

Round and round, until it began to form long stringy bits.

Round and round, until the stringy bits grew thinner and thinner.

Finally, Tally added the precious spider essence and the mixture instantly separated out into teeny tiny silver strands. It looked as though Tally had made a pot of angel hair.

Tiptoeing, they carried the pot through the kitchen, past the servants' hall and into the tapestry corridor. On the wall, just past the entrance to the ballroom, was the ancient tapestry.

'Don't worry,' she whispered to it, 'I would never

let those burglars steal you!'

Tally set the pot on the floor. From her pocket she drew out a tiny hook. The secret recipe had told her how to make it out of a needle. With sugar tongs, Tally lifted one of the cobweb strands and hooked it on to the needle, stretching the thread thinner and thinner until she could barely see it.

She climbed on to a stool and stuck a thread on the stone ceiling.

'There,' she said proudly, 'My first thread!'

It took Tally and Squill hours to make the web. They tried hard to copy the spider they'd seen in the book, but it was much more difficult than it looked. The pattern of the web was very complicated and at first Tally kept losing her place and dropping the thin thread. After a while she got the knack of it and before long she was moving quickly back and forth, curving the spider silk round and round and looping it over and under.

Bit by bit, they built a web.

Finally, as the clock struck midnight, they were finished. Tally stood back to look at it. The silk was so thin and light it almost disappeared. Only from one angle did it glint and sparkle in the moonlight.

'That's it!' cried Tally. 'The perfect trap.'

Now all they had to do was wait.

CHAPTER NINE

Tally yawned and stretched. Squill snuggled closer to her as he gently snored. The two friends were hidden in a little nook in the hallway, behind a large, ornate plant pot. They had been there for ages. Tally yawned again as she heard the clock in the hallway strike three. Maybe the burglars weren't coming. She sighed. All that work! She'd have to take the web down again before dawn, otherwise Mr Bood would tangle himself up in it. Tally bit her lip in frustration.

All at once the furry body next to her sat bolt upright. Squill's ears twitched.

'Did you hear something?' Tally whispered and Squill held up one claw for silence. Tally strained to listen. At first there was nothing. But then ...

A soft creak as the old dresser in the servants' hall was pushed along the floor. Someone had come through the malthouse tunnel! Tally heard the careful *tread, tread, tread* of feet across the servants' hallway. Her heart began to thump and Squill had to move away from the loud noise coming out of her chest so it didn't hurt his ears.

The squirrel peeked out from behind the nook. He darted back and gave Tally a little nod. The burglars were coming!

Tally could hear them talking now.

'Joe! Quick! Tapestry's this way.'

'Comin'. I's jes lookin' at the sofa.'

'Leave the sofa!'

'Jes one look, Harry ...'

Tally could hear the burglars sneaking into the ballroom. Then there was a loud squeaky noise.

'Joe! Stop jumpin' on the sofa.'

'But I likes it.'

'Joe!'

There was a clattering noise as Tally guessed that Harry was pulling Joe off the sofa and out of the ballroom.

'Come on. Stop messin'. You's ruinin' the plan. The tapestry is jes up there.'

Tally shrank back behind the pot plant as they came closer along the tapestry corridor, past the nook, past the stained-glass window, past Tally's hiding place. Her heart was beating fast, and for a moment she wondered if she was doing the right thing. Maybe she should have stayed safely tucked up in her sink, with Squill snuggled down next to her? But the burglars had nearly reached the web. Tally held her breath. She peered between the large leaves of the plant, using them as camouflage.

The burglars took another step … and another … and … 'Come on, come on,' whispered Tally.

She'd come this far for Lord Mollett. Her plan had to work.

'Hey!' cried one burglar.

'What's going on?' cried the other.

The burglars had walked right into the web.

'It's all sticky!' they shouted. They wriggled their arms and legs, trying to get free. They pushed forward, they pulled back, they twisted, they turned, but whatever they did, they couldn't escape.

'I's caught!'

'Me too!'

Tally stepped out from the nook. The web was nearly invisible. As the moonlight streamed in from the hallway window, it looked to Tally like the two burglars were blocked by a transparent wall. Then she saw the fine silver threads that were sticking them tight. She turned to Squill and grinned.

'Oi!'

'Stop!'

'Let me go!'

The burglars were getting louder and louder as they struggled. But every time they squirmed, the web tightened around their bodies. Soon, their shouts and cries filled the manor house. Squill quickly hid himself in Tally's pinafore pocket. They heard a rush of footsteps along the corridor. Tally stepped in front of the web as figures burst through a door.

'Stop!' she cried. 'Don't come any closer or you'll be caught, too.'

Three people stood in front of her in their pyjamas: Lord Mollett, Mrs Sneed and Mr Bood.

There was a clatter and then a fourth person appeared. It was Lady Mollett, taking small, careful steps. She was wearing an evening coat and a set of pearls over the top of her pyjamas. She'd even managed to pull on a pair of shoes, while Lord Mollett was wearing his bunny slippers.

All four of them glanced between Tally and the burglars. Lord Mollett's mouth dropped open and Lady Mollett gave a small squeal, pulling her evening coat tighter around her throat.

'What have you been doing, Tally?' Mrs Sneed snapped. 'It looks to me like you've Had Ideas!'

'Um ...' Everyone was staring at her. 'I ... I thought I'd catch the burglars.'

Mr Bood's mouth opened and closed, opened and closed.

Lord Mollett stepped forward.

'Tally! I knew you'd come up with a plan. This trap is fantastic! How did you make it?'

'Er ...' Tally knew the rules. She had to keep the

secret of the library. She thought quickly. 'I used all the spider webs I collected from the roses in the garden,' she answered, crossing her fingers behind her back.

'Very clever,' Lord Mollett breathed. He patted Tally on the shoulder.

Mr Bood coughed, 'Well, yes, it is a BIT clever,' he began. Tally was shocked. Was she about to receive some praise? 'But not as clever as MY plan. I was just about to put it into action myself, you know. Yes. I was just putting the finishing touches to the drawings.'

'Yes!' Mrs Sneed jumped into the conversation. 'And MY plan would have involved a lot less mess,' she sniffed, 'and a bit more cheese.'

'Hey!' yelled the thief called Harry. 'Can you get us down?'

'Too right,' added Joe. 'I needs a nap on your sofa.'

Lord Mollett and Mr Bood untangled the burglars, tearing through the spider web. The two men fell to the ground and out of their pockets fell:

one silver bear,

one spider brooch,

four emeralds,

one diamond ring,

three necklaces,

one watch,

a rolled-up painting

and half a chandelier.

'Where's the other half?' inquired Lord Mollett.

'I dropped it,' said Joe.

Lord Mollett bent down to rescue his silver bear and spider brooch. He turned them over carefully in his hands to check them and gave them a quick polish.

Then the lord of Mollett Manor turned to Tally.

'Thank you,' he said. Tally smiled. Lord Mollett

reached out and pinned something on her pinafore. Tally looked down and gasped. He had given her the spider brooch!

'You don't need to do that,' she spluttered.

'He certainly doesn't,' came Mrs Sneed's icy voice.

'I want to,' Lord Mollett said. Tally lit up inside like a firework. She tried hard to stop smiling. It would only annoy Mrs Sneed.

'Um … can we's have a cup of tea?' Harry asked.

'Yeah. You could bring it over to the sofa,' Joe suggested.

CHAPTER TEN

After their tea (and biscuits, and a second cup of tea, and a piece of apple cake) the burglars were escorted to the police station. As they left, they handed Lord Mollett their business card, just in case he ever needed anything stolen.

'We're always lookin' for windows of opportunity,' said Harry.

'Yeh. For our business.' Joe pointed to their matching red jumpers with the 'Snatch 'n' Grab' logo.

'Now, Tally,' Lord Mollett said, as they stood on the steps of Mollett Manor. 'I think you should come and visit me in my study every day. A brain like yours shouldn't go to waste. I think it would benefit from some French, and some history and—'

Tally could see Mrs Sneed's eyes narrowing with every word. Hastily, she jumped in. 'Mrs Sneed has already taught me a lot herself.' She crossed her fingers behind her back again, and hoped that such a big lie wouldn't matter.

'Ah!' Lord Mollett smiled and nodded his approval.

Mrs Sneed blushed and gazed down at her hands. 'Well, yes, that's true,' she said. 'But if the lord needs you then I can spare you briefly.' She brought her face close to Tally's. 'No having fun, though.'

'Oh, Tally!' Lady Mollett's shrill voice broke in. 'I need you to visit me, too. I have lots of things to organise. I need someone to teach me to tie my shoelaces, for a start. I can never remember what you do once you've made the bunny ears.' Tally hid a smile as she noticed Lady Mollett had somehow managed to tie her shoes together. No wonder she'd been taking such small, careful steps.

They all went inside and Tally shut the wooden doors of Mollett Manor behind them. The lord's belongings were back safe and the burglars would be taken care of. First thing in the morning Tally would fit a new lock to the old entranceway behind the dresser.

Tally smiled. No one had found out about the Secret Library and she'd managed to make everyone happy again.

'Not bad for a girl who sleeps in the kitchen sink,' Tally murmured to Squill. Her pocket wriggled in reply.

From then on life became a little easier for Tally. She had Squill, she had a new friend in Lord Mollett, and she had the Secret Library.

Every day, after her lessons in French and ancient history, Tally sneaked out to the Secret Library. There she read about all sorts of wonderful things, like how elephants find water, and how bumblebees fly, and what kind of poison is in venomous snakes. Sometimes, she would allow herself to read about baby animals and their mothers. Once, she was even able to watch a little orangutan clinging to its mother's side as they swung through the trees.

One afternoon in the Secret Library, Tally was reading about understanding different dog barks.[II] She opened the book and a little chihuahua floated out. It ran in circles around her feet and yapped playfully. Tally turned the page and a poodle appeared, growling a warning. Tally nodded, and committed the different barks to her memory. She was just about to turn the page again, when something caught her eye. In the right-hand margin was a pencil scribble. Tally peered closer.

What would a calling bark sound like?

[II] Dogs can vary their barks to mean different things. High-pitched sounds generally mean the dog is excited. Low-pitched sounds could be a sign of aggression.

Make megaphone?

How can I change my voice to get it right?

Tally frowned. Who had written that note? One of the Secret Keepers before her? A thrill ran through her. Squill tapped her on the hand. He wanted to know what the writing said. In a shaky voice, Tally began to read out loud.

'What would a— Oh!'

Tally's heart skipped a beat. Out of the book rose a hologram. It was a young girl, about Tally's age. She had curly blonde hair and a collection of

bracelets on her wrist. Tally knew her instantly. It was Ma. Ma as a girl!

The second Tally stopped reading, the image disappeared. Frantically, she cast her eyes down the page to find the note again.

'What would a calling bark ...'

Tally read Ma's notes aloud, over and over again, watching the girl frowning in concentration as she wrote in the margin.

'Oh, Ma,' Tally cried. 'I miss you!' But the other girl didn't seem to hear. She ran her fingers over Ma's precious handwriting. Her heart felt like it would break. 'I wish you were here,' she whispered.

But the image was gone.

'Ma was a Secret Keeper too,' Tally said to Squill, as they turned to leave the library. 'That's how she knew about the song and the stones. She brought me to the cliffs that day to teach me how to become one too.' A smile spread across her face as she reached for her friend's paw.

'I'm going to find out more about
my mother, Squill,' she said firmly.
'And the Secret Library is
going to help me.'

Acknowledgements

My thanks go to Eve White — who has supported me right from the start; Karen and Becca for all their help kicking the story into shape; and to James Brown for his fantastic illustrations. Also to the Scattered Authors' Society — I *could* do it without you, but it would be a lot less fun. — Abie Longstaff

Many thanks to Jodie Hodges and Emily Talbot at United Agents and the wonderful, creative team at Little, Brown — in particular, Sophie Burdess, who loves foil too. Mostly, my appreciation goes to Abie for writing such a beautifully spun, intricately woven story. — James Brown

About the Author

ABIE LONGSTAFF is the eldest of six children and grew up in Australia, Hong Kong and France. She knows all about squabbling and bossing younger sisters around so she began her career as a barrister. She started writing when her children were born. Her books include *The Fairytale Hairdresser* series and *The Magic Potions Shop* books. She has a life-long love of fairy tales and mythology and her work is greatly influenced by these themes.

Abie got the idea for the *Tally and Squill* books from her parents' house in France. The house is big and old, with lots of rooms and outbuildings. In one of the bedrooms, there is a secret entrance hidden in a fireplace. It leads to a room that was used by the French Resistance during the war. It was the perfect idea for a book!

Abie lives with her family by the seaside in Hove.

About the Illustrator

Inspired by a school visit from Anthony Browne
at the age of eight, JAMES BROWN has wanted
to illustrate ever since. Having won the SCBWI's
Undiscovered Voices 2014 competition, he has
illustrated the *Elspeth Hart* series and two of his own
Archie and George books, as well as writing two picture
books which are published in 2017. James comes
from Nottingham and has two cheeky daughters
who usually take off with his favourite crayons.

Find out what happens next in
TALLY AND SQUILL'S adventure . . .

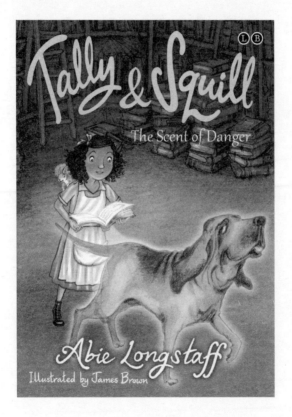

MAY 2017